Why We Left

I Remember
VIETNAM

Jo Matthews

Photographs by Tim Page

RAINTREE
STECK-VAUGHN
PUBLISHERS
The Steck-Vaughn Company

Austin, Texas

© 1995, text, Steck-Vaughn Company

Published by Raintree Steck-Vaughn Publishers, an imprint of Steck-Vaughn Company

Editors: Sally Matthews, Edith Vann
Designer: Peter Bennett
Cover Design: Joyce Spicer
Illustrator: David Burroughs
Consultant: Nguyen Vu Long

Library of Congress Cataloging-in-Publication Data

Matthews, Jo.
    I Remember Vietnam / Jo Matthews/ photographs by Tim Page.
        p.   cm. — (Why we left)
    Includes index.
    ISBN 0-8114-5605-6
    1. Vietnam — Juvenile literature.
I. Page, Tim.   II. Title.   III. Series.
DS556.3.M38   1995
959.7—dc20   94-21854
                                 CIP   AC

Printed and bound in Belgium

1 2 3 4 5 6 7 8 9 0 PR 99 98 97 96 95 94

Contents

Introduction

My name is Han. I come from Vietnam. My family and I came to live in the West with thousands of other refugees. Many of us had to leave Vietnam during and after the war. We escaped by crossing the sea in boats. That is why we are often known as the Vietnamese boat people.

Like all refugees, I now have two homes. They are very different. I want you to come with me to Vietnam. Come to the mighty Mekong River, the cities and the temples, and the beautiful country. In this way, you can learn about Vietnam. And you can help me remember my old home.

Refugees are people who leave their homes because it is not safe to live there. Millions of people all over the world have been forced to leave their countries. They have fled from civil wars, earthquakes, floods, being poor, and lack of food.

Welcome to Vietnam

Vietnam is in Southeast Asia. It has its own language and alphabet. Vietnamese is a bit like Chinese. In both languages, a word can have many different meanings. The meaning depends on how the word is said. In Vietnamese the word *ma* can mean "cheek," "horse," "ghost," "coffin," "bush," or "but."

There are nearly 70 million people in Vietnam. Seventy-eight percent live in the country. Twenty-two percent live in the towns and cities.

The economy of Vietnam depends mainly on agriculture. Most of the people earn their living farming or fishing.

Vietnam is called "the land of two rice baskets." It is shaped like two rice baskets hanging on a farmer's carrying pole (left). Such baskets are used to carry rice and other foods to the markets (right). Rice is Vietnam's most important crop.

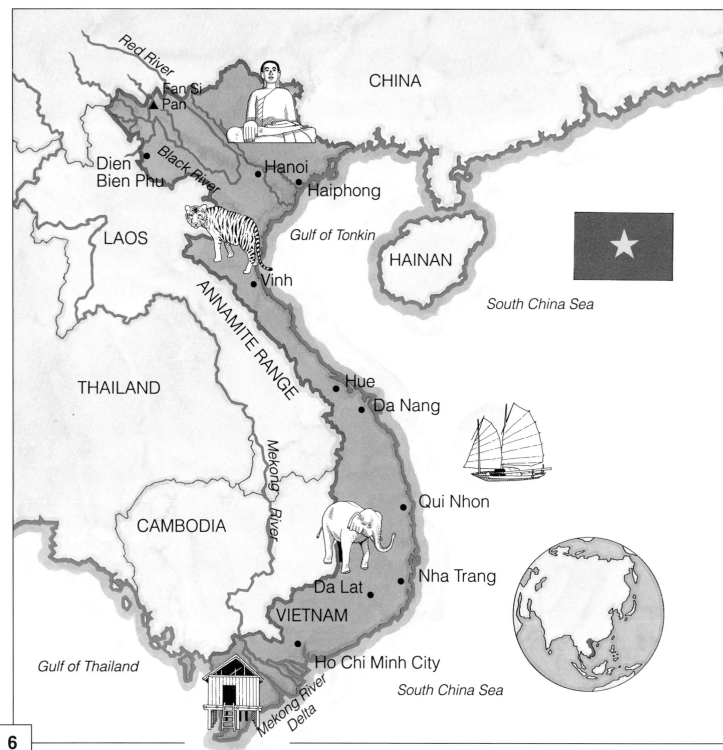

Red River

Fan Si
▲ Pan

CHINA

Dien
Bien Phu

Black River

Hanoi

Haiphong

LAOS

Gulf of Tonkin

HAINAN

Vinh

South China Sea

THAILAND

ANNAMITE RANGE

Hue

Da Nang

Mekong River

Qui Nhon

CAMBODIA

Nha Trang

Da Lat

VIETNAM

Gulf of Thailand

Ho Chi Minh City

South China Sea

Mekong River
Delta

The Country

Vietnam is a long, thin country. It hugs the eastern coast of Southeast Asia. Laos, Cambodia, and China border one side. The South China Sea is on the other.

It has a long chain of mountains called the Annamite Range. It runs all the way down the western side of the country. The highest mountain is Fan Si Pan. It is one-third the height of Mount Everest. Vietnam has lost many of its rain forests. Still they cover over a third of the country. The largest rivers are the Red River in the north and the Mekong in the south.

Most people live in the rich lowlands near the rivers and along the coast. But some still live in the mountains.

Vietnam is a very beautiful country. Although it is fairly small, it has many different types of lands. There are high mountains, thick forests, and wide, winding rivers. The rich lowlands are patched with rice paddies. The coastlines have palm trees and white, sandy beaches.

Weather and Wildlife

Vietnam has a tropical climate. That means it is hot and damp for most of the year. The weather is influenced by monsoons. These are winds that bring rain. In Vietnam, they bring very heavy rain in the summer (right). They bring lighter rain in the winter. Most of Vietnam has only two seasons. This is unlike many other countries, which also have spring and autumn.

It is this hot, wet weather that makes Vietnam so green and fertile. It is ideal for growing rice and keeping the rain forests alive. However, it also causes floods and typhoons. These can do a lot of damage.

Vietnam's forests contain many exotic plants, from rare orchids to poisonous giant sack trees.

There are also many wild animals, including tigers, monkeys, bears, peacocks, and snakes. Snakes are also farmed in Vietnam. Their venom is taken out (or milked). It is used to make a cure for snakebites.

The Vietnamese People

Vietnam began as a small country in the north over 4,000 years ago. About 200 B.C. China took over Vietnam and ruled it for over 1,000 years. Many Chinese people went to live there. The country slowly grew bigger. It took in other people toward the south, like the Montagnards and Khmers. Together these groups make up the Vietnamese people of today.

Beginning in the nineteenth century, the French ruled Vietnam for many years. After they left, in 1954, the country was divided into North Vietnam and South Vietnam. This led to years of bitter war between the people. They were not united again until 1976.

A variety of clothes (right) reflect some of the different origins of Vietnamese people.

11

Vietnam's most important festival is the Tet New Year. This takes place in January or early February. It is celebrated in a similar way to Christmas, which Christians celebrate all over the world.

It is a time for feasts, firecracker displays, gift-giving, and decorating our houses. Instead of a Christmas tree (right), we buy colorful blossoming trees from the Tet flower markets (above).

Our Beliefs

There are lots of different beliefs in Vietnam. Most people follow a mixture of old and new religions. The ancient worship of animal spirits and ancestors has been combined with common faiths like Buddhism. Buddhism is the largest religion in Vietnam. Religion is not popular with the ruling Communist Party. It has closed down temples all over the country. But many people still have strong religious beliefs.

The Vietnamese also have many superstitions. For example, many of us put mirrors on our front doors. We believe that dragons trying to get into our house will be scared away by seeing themselves.

The people are always careful not to point their feet toward the Buddha when they pray. Pointing your feet at people is thought to be very rude in Vietnam.

Also, you should never touch a person's head in public. It is believed that this will harm the spirit that lives there.

Family Life

Families in Vietnam are usually very big. We share a home with many of our relatives. This is called an extended family. It includes about three generations or more. Families are very close, eating, worshiping, and working together (right).

As children, we must be obedient. We must do as we are told by anyone older than we are. Today, most children go to school. Our parents used to arrange our marriages. But now we usually choose our own partners.

In recent years, many people have left their villages for large cities. This is beginning to change common family life in Vietnam.

We eat with chopsticks rather than knives and forks (left). We eat rice with fish, meat, vegetables, and spicy sauces.

Leisure

Vietnamese people like to relax and enjoy themselves after a hard day at work. They love poems, music, dance, and plays. Many are very old and handed down from parents to children. Many young people enjoy pop music. Children often watch puppet shows. The Vietnamese are also great readers, so books are very popular, too. Vietnam has many newspapers and magazines. Some people also have radios or televisions. In villages, people often listen to radio programs over loudspeakers. Many watch jointly-owned televisions in groups.

We love to enjoy a good day at the races. Horse racing is popular in Europe and America. And camel racing is common in many Arab countries. But we like to race elephants.

Traditional martial arts, like Tai Chi (above), are very popular in Vietnam. The state encourages daily exercise. People of all ages do Tai Chi to relax and keep fit.

However, Western sports such as pool have become popular, especially with the young people (left).

Many people have small covered boats called *sampans.* They often serve as home, transportation, and floating food stand, all in one (above).

Every day, people set off in boats full of goods. They go to the floating markets (right). Here, they can buy and sell all kinds of products. These include fish, fruit, vegetables, and rice.

Life Along the Rivers

Two huge rivers are the Mekong and Red rivers. They cut across the country, leaving thousands of miles of waterways behind them. This is where most Vietnamese people live. Some fish in the rivers. Others grow rice in rich, wet fields called rice paddies.

There are few good roads in Vietnam. Most people travel and move their goods along the rivers. Whole towns are built on the water. They have floating markets. There are houses on stilts, tall posts that keep them safe from floods.

Many people who live along the rivers fish for a living. Fish is the second most important food in Vietnam. Tuna, mackerel, sardines, and shellfish, such as oysters and shrimp, are caught. They fish in coastal and inland waters.

The fishing industry needs more boats. Many were used by refugees to escape from Vietnam. So, many have to fish from the shores and riverbanks (right).

City Life

Hanoi, in the north, is the capital of Vietnam. However, the largest city is Ho Chi Minh City, in the south. This was called Saigon until the end of the war.

Life can be very hard in the cities. They had a lot of damage during the war. Like many cities all over the world, they have overcrowding and housing shortages.

City dwellers face a desperate struggle to find houses, jobs, and food. The living conditions are bad. Many people have no running water or electricity.

Food is in very short supply. It is rationed to make sure that everybody gets something to eat. The government also provides meals in big food halls. Most people eat there during the day.

The Vietnamese currency is called the dong. This is a 5,000 dong note (right).

There are very few cars in Vietnam. Most people ride bicycles to get around from place to place. They use bicycles to carry their goods to the markets (left and above).

In developed countries, trucks are usually used to carry and deliver goods (below).

Farming in Vietnam

Away from the rivers and the cities, people from the Khmer group are farmers. They still farm the land in the same way that their ancestors did. They live in villages, in houses made of straw, palm leaves, or wood. They farm small patches of land that they own. Their main crop is rice. But coffee, cassava, cotton, and corn are grown, too.

Over the years, the Communist Party has forced many farmers to leave their villages. They work on large state-run communes. On communes, farmers live and work together. They cannot own their own land or sell their own crops. This is very unpopular. Now the government has allowed many farmers to return to their villages. They can farm in their usual way.

Farmers wear practical cotton shirts and pants. They also wear cone-shaped hats, which protect them from the sun (right).

22

In Vietnam rice is grown in paddy fields. This means that it is kept in water until it is harvested. The farmers often have to cut ditches from rivers to keep the fields wet. This is called irrigation. The farmers harvest their crops by hand (left). They use water buffalo to plow their fields (top). In more developed countries, jobs like these would be done with machinery (above).

Living in the Mountains

High in the mountains live the hill people called Montagnards. There are 39 different Montagnard tribes. Each has its own language, customs, and way of life.

These highland people hunt in the forests and fish in the mountain streams. They have a partly nomadic form of agriculture. This means that they clear a small plot of land. They farm it until the soil is worn out. Then they move on to another piece of land. They grow various crops, including rice, soybeans, cinnamon, tea, tobacco, cotton, fruit trees, and bamboo.

The government is trying to improve health and education for the Montagnards. They are the most separated of the Vietnamese people.

Mountain people live in small villages. Their houses are made of bamboo. They are built on stilts (left) to protect them from rain and wild animals. There are no roads. They walk everywhere, carrying goods in baskets on their backs (far left). The women are skilled at embroidery and weaving. This can be seen in their clothes (right).

Why I'm Here

After years of control by the French, most Vietnamese people wanted independence. Some wanted communism, and others wanted nationalism. So, in 1954, Vietnam was divided. The communist north was led by Ho Chi Minh and the nationalist south, by Bao Dai. But some people still wanted a united Vietnam, and war broke out. Other countries became involved. China supplied arms to the north. America sent in troops to protect the south from communism. After years of fighting and millions of casualties, the north won. It took over the whole country in 1976.

Since then, life has been extremely hard for the southerners who opposed communism. This is one reason why over a million of us have left Vietnam. We are seeking safety in other countries.

Thousands risked their lives fleeing from Vietnam in small boats. Many who succeeded are still in camps in Hong Kong, waiting for new homes.

My Future

I've lived in the West for a few years now.
I feel like I belong here. I speak English, go to
school, and have many new friends. It is
important that I can say what I think without
getting into trouble. That is a very special thing.
I am happy in my new home. But a part of
me will always be in Vietnam.

Slowly, Vietnam is recovering from its
wars. It is rebuilding and offering a better
future for the children of today (left).
Soon, I hope, the bad memories will fade.
I hope the Vietnamese people will learn
to trust one another again.

I'm glad that Vietnam has survived
such troubled times. One day, I hope to
visit the beautiful mountains and mighty
Mekong once more.

Tam Biet (Goodbye)!

Fact File

Land and People

Official name: Công hoa xâ hôi chu nghia Viêt
(Socialist Republic of Vietnam)

National language: Vietnamese

Population: 70 million

Cities

Capital city: Hanoi

Other major cities: Ho Chi Minh City (formerly Saigon), Haiphong

Weather

Climate: Tropical monsoon region

Landmarks

Area: 128,052 square miles (331,653 sq km)

Most important rivers: Mekong, Red River

Highest mountain: Fan Si Pan 10,312 feet (3,143 m) above sea level

Culture

Main religions: Buddhist (55%), Taoist, Confucian, Roman Catholic, Islam

Ethnic groups: Vietnamese (85%), Montagnards, Chinese, Khmer

Literacy rate: 94 percent

Government

Form of government: Socialist Republic

Head of state: President

Eligibility to vote: All citizens 18 years and over

Food and Farming

Major crops: Rice, sugarcane, cassava, sweet potatoes, rubber

Trade and Industry

Employment: Agriculture, forestry and fishing (70%), industry and commerce (9%), military service (5%)

Mineral resources: Coal, phosphates, iron, manganese

Industries: Food processing, textiles, cement, fertilizer

Currency: Dong

Major exports: Coal, peanuts, rubber, tea, and bamboo products

Major imports: Petroleum, medicines, machinery, motor vehicles, and food

Index

Photographic Credits:
Special thanks to Tim Page/Eye Ubiquitous for supplying the pictures for this book. Additional pictures from:
Front cover: Frank Spooner Pictures; Front cover inset, p. 3, p. 21 (bottom), p. 29: Roger Vlitos; p. 12 (bottom): Spectrum; p. 23 (bottom): Charles de Vere.